OCTOBER GHOSTS
AND
AUTUMN DREAMS
MORE POEMS FOR HALLOWEEN

Praise for *October Ghosts and Autumn Dreams: More Poems for Halloween*

"K. A. Opperman's second book of Halloween poetry isn't just a celebration of that most beloved of dark festivals—it's a hypnotic dream weaver that cocoons the unwary (but fortunate) reader in a rich autumnal spell made up of pumpkins, the risen dead, and Halloween's special enchantment. This is a book to pick up anytime in the year when you need a dose of magic."

— **Lisa Morton**, author of
Trick or Treat: A History of Halloween

"Calling all Halloween lovers, children of October, Pumpkin Kings— October Ghosts and Autumn Dreams stirs together folklore and storytelling to evoke the sense that we are elsewhere—in the past perhaps, or submerged in some collective autumnal memory. Open this book after dark, listen to the wind rage outside, and read—to yourself, to your children, to whoever might be listening in the shadows."

— **Lesley Pratt Bannatyne**, author of *Halloween: An American Holiday, an American History*

"K. A. Opperman captures the bittersweet joy of Halloween and the sadness of its passing. Here are poems of childhood and poems of its loss. Captured by a lyricist with a clear, pronounced love for his labor, October Ghosts is Opperman the most at home, spooky, haunted and candle-lit though that home may be. Here is the poet's joy, laid bare and generously shared for readers young and old alike."

— **S. L. Edwards**, author of
Whiskey and Other Unusual Ghosts

Praise for *October Ghosts and Autumn Dreams: More Poems for Halloween*

"K. A. Opperman has done it again as his new book of poems opens a creaking gate that invites you into the world of Halloween. Pumpkins and black cats frolic beneath the moon as these poems paint autumn vignettes in the head of the reader. If Halloween is a state of mind these verses will whisk you there on an enchanted broom in a whirlwind of autumn leaves. October Ghosts and Autumn Dreams: More Poems for Halloween does not disappoint and is the perfect companion to Opperman's previous *Past the Glad and Sunlit Season: Poems for Halloween*. This book will cast its spell on your dark Halloween heart!"

— **Mickie Mueller**, author of *Llewellyn's Little Book of Halloween*

"K. A. Opperman's *October Ghosts & Autumn Dreams: More Poems for Halloween* is an enchanting dive into all the beauty that encapsulates the autumnal spirit. From catchy rhythms to recite while carving jack-o-lanterns in 'Carver's Rhyme' to a well-researched look into Appalachian customs in Appalachian Halloween, every line is beautifully crafted and sure to be appreciated by anyone who is a fan of the spooky season!"

— **Heather Moser**, Producer of *Small Town Monsters*

"Opperman's poems paint vivid pictures of autumn nights filled with nocturnal wonder. This collection is a heartfelt love letter to the season of dead leaves and glaring jack-o'-lanterns that imbues the reader with magical feelings of Halloweens past."

— **Curtis M. Lawson**, author of *Devil's Night*

Praise for *Past the Glad and Sunlit Season: Poems for Halloween*

"...[K. A. Opperman] is the gifted descendent of poets ranging from Poe to Walter Scott to Robert Burns, all of whom understood that Halloween's deliciously dark mood may be best served by poetry."

— From the Preface by **Lisa Morton**, author of *Trick or Treat: A History of Halloween*

"K. A. Opperman's poems evoke both the dark chill of late October and the warmth of a cottage fireside. He captures a time outside of time, an otherworld populated by Pumpkin Kings and haunted souls who wander the edges of our consciousness begging to come inside. The book is a heartfelt incantation to mysteries of Halloween."

— **Lesley Pratt Bannatyne**, author of *Halloween: An American Holiday, an American History*

"Halloweens past have often been preserved through verse and this collection brings that tradition forward, linking the heritage of old customs with the present and beyond. In the tradition of Burns or Poe, K. A. Opperman's *Past the Glad and Sunlit Season: Poems for Halloween* captures the spirit of the shadow and stirs up deep memories and hidden secrets of this time of the year. These visions of All Hallows' Eve are sure to enchant and whisk the reader away to a world of crisp autumn leaves, brimming with magic. The poems within this collection are steeped in folklore and perfectly reflect the ambiance of Halloween. This book will become your treasured new Halloween tradition."

— **Mickie Mueller**, author of *Llewellyn's Little Book of Halloween*

Praise for *Past the Glad and Sunlit Season: Poems for Halloween*

"K.A. Opperman has gifted us a varied gathering of lovely, intelligent poems that swell from a passion for the magical black and orange season. Beautiful and evocative, the works are rich in imagery and mood, composed of intriguing rhyme schemes and word choices. Reading this collection made me think of the noble poetry of old, and the subject could not appeal to me more. *Past the Glad and Sunlit Season* is a treasure from a superb wordsmith whose love for the great season burns brighter than a thousand jack-o'-lanterns. I hereby dub Mr. Opperman the poet laureate of Halloween."

— **Scott Thomas**, author of *The Sea of Ash*

"Follow the flickering orange light into the darkness beyond Summer's End, and pay court to the Pumpkin King. . . . K. A. Opperman's passion for Halloween burns as brightly as Jack's fabled lantern. That, combined with his uncanny metrical precision, is a potent recipe for verse-magick that is as haunting as it is darkly delightful."

— **Adam Bolivar**, author of *The Lay of Old Hex*

"*Past the Glad and Sunlit Season* is a cornucopia of autumnal delights. At turns whimsical and sombre, K. A. Opperman's Halloween poems serve as fine evocations of that season of mist, fire, and scythe."

— **Richard Gavin**, author of *Sylvan Dread: Tales of Pastoral Darkness*

"All hail the Pumpkin King, aka K. A. Opperman! Those of us who love Halloween in all its guises will be delighted by this collection of seasonal poetry."

— **Denise Dumars**, author of *The Dark Archetype: Exploring the Shadow Side of the Divine*

Also by K. A. Opperman

OCTOBER GHOSTS
AND
AUTUMN DREAMS
MORE POEMS FOR HALLOWEEN

K. A. OPPERMAN
WITH A FOREWORD BY
ADAM BOLIVAR

ILLUSTRATIONS BY
DAN SAUER

JACKANAPES PRESS

For Ashley
my pumpkin patch partner

CONTENTS

I. PUMPKIN COUNTRY

II. HALLOWEEN DREAMS

III. AUTUMN MEMORIES

ILLUSTRATIONS

FOREWORD

THE ORANGE AND BLACK LAND

K. A. Opperman has chosen Halloween as an object of religious devotion. And I do not use that word frivolously. It is truly a religion to him. Well, why shouldn't it be? Of all the holidays of the year, Halloween is the most mystical, the one most shrouded in mystery. It is not a celebration of light and life in the way that Yule and Easter are; quite the contrary, Halloween heralds the coming of darkness and death. On the surface, it is a night to be feared. Yet it is also the time when we are closest to loved ones who have died, to long-forgotten ancestors, a time when we remember that death too is part of life's journey. One day, we must all enter into that undiscovered country, and we hope that those who come after us may conjure our memory.

So Halloween, after all, plays a crucial part in the turn of the year, one that is woefully overlooked.

But K. A. Opperman does not overlook it. He immerses himself in the symbols of Halloween: black cats, the full moon, bats, witches on broomsticks, trick-or-treating, pumpkins... Especially pumpkins. Opperman has seized upon this particular symbol with an especial fervor. The majority of the poems in this volume concern pumpkins: their cultivation, their aesthetic qualities, their uses as foodstuffs, and their macabre metamorphosis into jack-o'-lanterns on the advent of the holy night.

The jack-o'-lantern is an embodiment of the legend of Stingy Jack, who, unwelcome in Heaven or Hell, was forced to wander through the darkness for all eternity with only a demonic coal in a lantern to light his lonely way. Jack's grotesque grin was once crudely cut into a hollowed-out turnip or swede and lit from within by a candle. Since the nineteenth century, the more easily carved pumpkin has come to replace the intractable root vegetables of the Old World—an American innovation which has left an indelible stamp on the holiday.

Likewise, K. A. Opperman himself has left a lasting mark on Halloween, by sheer force of will and the relentless charm of his poems, many of which are written as folkish chants reminiscent of old charms to make your garden grow. (And make your garden grow they will. I have it on good authority.) In his longer-lined compositions, the poet masterfully maintains a meticulous meter and rhyme, a precious skill in this era when free verse is the norm. Opperman has no small reputation as a formal poet, and his scrupulous scansion evokes the sort of Halloween poems which were popular in the nineteenth and early twentieth centuries—to be read aloud in the dark by a crackling hearth-fire, a cup of hot apple cider in hand to chase away the chill of the encroaching winter. There is a palpable longing in these poems

   October Ghosts and Autumn Dreams

for a bygone age, a time when we were more attuned to the subtle rhythms of the earth, and still held reverence for the pagan spirits which linger in the corn and the woods. On Halloween we return to this time, if for only one night, and it is up to us whether we bolt the door and cower in our beds, or join the phantasms in their midnight revels.

So venture into the corn maze of K. A. Opperman's imagination. You will not be disappointed by what you find there. There are those who call him the Pumpkin King, and who am I to dispute this title? And who knows? You may be persuaded to join him in Pumpkin Country, the orange and black land where it is always October, where pumpkins grow as big as the harvest moon, and conical-hatted witches dance around a bonfire with a horned god. Let me open the gate for you...

—Adam Bolivar
Portland, Oregon
Lammas, 2021

INTRODUCTION

SONGS FROM A HALLOWED HYMNAL

Once again, the long, hot summer looms before me, and once again, I find myself dreaming of the colorful, enchanted land waiting just to the other side of it. I have written another book of Halloween poems to share with you, and now I will strive to say a few words by way of introduction. In a way, this introductory text plays a role similar to the summer season in regards to autumn: a transitory passage we must get through before indulging in the October incantations to follow. But, like summer, I will see if I can make this magical, warm, and bright, but also brief, so as not to delay the harvest festivities.

I never planned to write a second book of Halloween poems, but as with the first book, I just kept writing them, and writing them, and soon, one thing led to another. This is, as it seems to me, a collection of more of the same—a direct continuation of *Past the Glad and Sunlit Season*. Together, these two books comprise one hundred poems, and that was no accident—one hundred poems celebrating the Halloween season and the candlelit mysteries of October.

This collection is divided into three sections, ranging in subject and mood from the lighthearted and fun to the more melancholy and serious. Among the first section, especially, may be found several poems that may prove suitable for children. For so many of us, our love of Halloween is deeply rooted in our original childhood experiences of this most wondrous holiday and its peculiar autumn magic, so these poems should hopefully speak not only to the young, but to the young at heart as well. Toward the end of the book, however, old souls may find that certain somber music that ravens sometimes croak at dusk, and that dead leaves scrape from the chilly sidewalk on their aimless windblown course.

* * *

The previous collection has already achieved a level of popularity beyond what I ever could have hoped for, and I can only hope that this book will meet with a similar level of approval in the Halloween community and beyond. My purpose in writing these books is to encapsulate and share my deeply devoted love of the Halloween season with others who feel the same way as I do, so it warms my heart to know that, so far, I seem to be succeeding. In times past, I used to divide my efforts between Halloween verses and other horror-oriented poems, but nowadays, quaint rhymes involving Halloween are virtually all that I write. Whenever I set pen to paper, a spirited pumpkin paean is not long to follow.

I consider it one of my highest goals in life to be forever true to the time-honored ways of Halloween, and to help spread the autumnal magic that flames in my heart to as many other October souls as possible. Nothing fills me with more of a sense of purpose, and nothing strikes me as a more sacred task. With these heartfelt words, filtered through a colorful candy-wrapper lens of childhood memories, and mingled with auspicious present-day experiences, I hope to illuminate and deepen for you the eternal magic of Halloween.

The hay-bale in the pumpkin-patch is my pulpit, and this collection is a new chapter in my jack-o'-lantern-embossed gold and orange hymnal. A scarecrow creaks in the wind, and a raven eyes you inquisitively, inviting you to join our strange congregation. Pick your perfect pumpkin, take your prickly seat on a bundle of sun-bleached hay, and close your eyes as these cinnamon-scented spells waft over you, carried on a wistful autumn wind. Hear the dead leaves falling— hear their summer-crisp rasp as yesterday fades into a memory and is blown over the sunset fields of forever...

The sun has now set; bats and owls are stirring. The wind has grown colder, and your heart has grown darker. But there is light—a light in the pumpkin you have carven a ghoulish face upon, while deep in reverie. This light flickers in your heart, too—a flame, fed by candied apples and cider, and that particular brand of danger and adventure that is to be found on an October night. Take your jack-o'-lantern in hand, and begin your journey through the autumn darkness...

October Ghosts await you.

—K. A. Opperman
Corona, California
4 September 2021

I

PUMPKIN COUNTRY

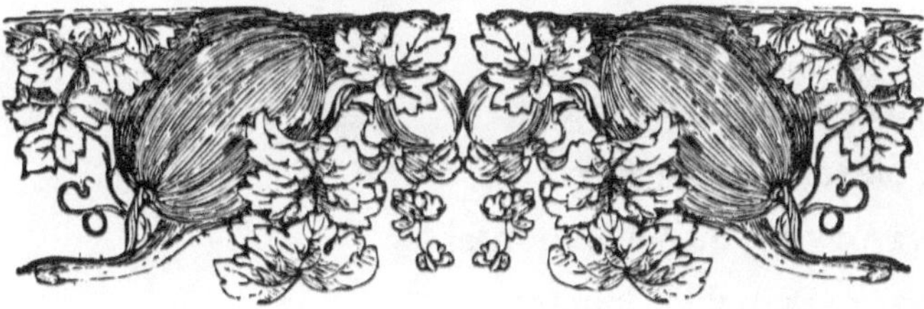

Pumpkin Country

The town has faded far behind,
A scarecrow marks your entry
As down an autumn road you find
The fabled Pumpkin Country.

It is a land of rolling hills,
And farmlands never-ending—
Of quiet creeks and watermills,
And pathways gently wending.

Whichever way you chance to look
In that enchanted haven,
Are pumpkins placed in every nook,
And many a skulking raven.

If you a jack-o'-lantern seek,
Or pie to fill your pantry,
Away, away, you ought to sneak—
Away to Pumpkin Country.

The Greatest Gift

A pumpkin is the greatest gift
That anyone can give;
They give the soul a little lift,
Beloved by all who live.

To see them huddled in the patch,
Or glowing on the wall,
Holds magic nothing else can match
For children big and small.

Pumpkin Spell

I have a pure and simple wish,
A wish that I now tell:
To grow a pumpkin—swirl and swish!—
I cast my pumpkin spell.

I trace around the candle-flame
Its grinning shape, compel
The orange glow to form my aim—
I cast my pumpkin spell.

The Star of All My Garden

The star of all my garden
Is a sprawling pumpkin plant,
Whose jack-o'-lanterns harden
Their orange glow to grant.

A yellow flower crowns it,
A soft and fallen star,
Which, when the twilight drowns it,
Draws faeries from afar.

Appalachian Halloween

A hex-sign guards the homestead's verge,
A magic carven star,
While autumn moans her mournful dirge,
A-sighing near and far.

Inside, the kids cut spooky shapes
From paper orange and black;
Their scherenschnitte gaily drapes
The house from front to back.

Dumb Supper afterward is held
By dressed up maidens fair;
Their suitors' fetches are compelled
To take an empty chair.

Then backward through the cabin door,
Into the dark, they walk,
While witches o'er the mountains soar,
And jack-o'-lanterns talk.

Carver's Rhyme

All I need's a knife and a spoon,
And I'll have your jack-o'-lantern soon.
Scrape the guts, carve the face,
And put the candle in its place.

The Parade Lantern

This torch, my child, grows heavy in my hand,
For I am weary with the weight of years—
Take up this tarnished, pumpkin-shapen brand,
And bear it forth as night's first star appears.

Hold up this humble scepter sparked with flame,
And hold parade all down this autumn street—
Make of your march a gladsome, goblin game,
As in the dim, lost days of trick-or-treat.

In the Name of Halloween

Raise your pennants, hold parade,
Beat your festive tambourine,
Keep your lanterns well displayed
In the name of Halloween.

Don your mask and trick-or-treat,
Eat some candy, count thirteen,
Crunch some leaves beneath your feet
In the name of Halloween.

Host a party, play a game,
Break your everyday routine,
Gaze into the grinning flame
In the name of Halloween.

Bob for apples, bake some cakes,
Tell us what the fortunes mean,
Every ghoul and ghost awakes
In the name of Halloween.

Crepe Paper Patterns

Repeating pumpkins in a weird motif,
Black cats and witches nigh without relief,
The webs of spiders, owl, bat, and leaf—
Crepe paper patterns, sheaf on crinkly sheaf!

So too these poems bear the same parade
Of autumn symbols playfully arrayed—
Small orange paintings on each page displayed,
Yet writ in words, a witching serenade.

Cat-o'-Lantern

I carved my pumpkin like a cat,
With whiskers, nose, and perky ears;
I set it on my welcome mat,
As people do when twilight nears.

It wasn't long—the doorbell rang—
And who should stand upon my stair
But thirteen cats, a green-eyed gang
As black as pitch, or witches' hair.

I poured them out a pan of milk,
And happily, they lapped it up—
But mirrored there, with skin like silk,
Were pretty witches crouched to sup.

'October ghosts and autumn dreams,'
I whispered as they slipped away—
But in the cat-o'-lantern's gleams,
My mind more tricks began to play.

I thought I saw them stand on twos,
In pointed crimson caps encrowned—
I surely had begun to snooze,
The way those sneaky felines clowned.

A grinning, fanged, grimalkin moon
Soon rose, invoked by yowling cry,
And like a draping crepe festoon—
A chain of witches crossed the sky.

Time for Halloween

Black cats and bats and witch's hats—
It's time for Halloween!
Orange pumpkins grin and ghosts begin
Descending on the scene.

Red devils dance and skeletons glance
With glowing eyes of green;
In haunted house nest owl and mouse—
It's time for Halloween.

Witch's Candy

Lollipops with pretty swirls—
Black for boys, and orange for girls—
Ribbon bows with bouncing curls—
This is the witch's candy.

Dipped in poison, dripping green,
Later dried and rendered clean...
Polished to a sugary sheen,
They look so fine and dandy.

Sparkling wrappers, rainbow-bright,
Hide her cauldron's taint from sight.
Children snatch them with delight,
And add them to their baskets.

Done up like a lollipop,
Lace, black bows, and copper top,
Watching from her candy shop,
The witch prepares their caskets...

The Pumpkin Juggler

There is a clown that juggles all day long,
And jack-o'-lanterns are his chosen ball.
When from the circus floats a strange, sad song,
The fool performs, and lets no pumpkin fall.

On Halloween, his unicycle squeaks
Down autumn roads where smiling pumpkins shine;
The black and orange jester ever seeks
To steal more pumpkins for his strange design.

The Three Pretty Pumpkins

Gourdelia, Gourda, and Gourdette
Were pumpkin sprites, a perfect set—
The prettiest pumpkins in the patch,
With dresses, shoes, and hats to match.

Their shoes were bright and shiny green,
Their dresses flashed with leafy sheen;
Their pumpkin hats, complete with stems,
Encrowned their curls like orange gems.

The human-folk who came to pick
A pumpkin only saw a trick:
They only saw the pumpkins three,
All looking normal as can be.

But underneath the quaint mirage,
Their magic faerie camouflage,
The pumpkin triplets primped and preened,
They puffed and posed, and slyly leaned.

Each sister wished to be the one
That would be chosen—O what fun
To ride a wagon through the grass,
Pulled homeward by a human lass.

Gourdette was judged to be most fair,
Gourdette with gorgeous, orange hair.
They plucked her up, and plopped her down,
And then they headed back to town.

Gourdelia, and Gourda, too,
Were sad to see her go, it's true—
And yet, they knew their turn would come,
And so the sprites were not so glum.

Gourdette, so glamorous, waved goodbye,
Her voice soon lost to raven's cry—
But Gourda noticed something strange,
And soon her mood began to change.

She noticed that the daughter's dress
Was made with pumpkin print, no less—
But on each one was carved a grin,
The jack-o'-lantern's wicked kin.

And then she knew Gourdette would be
Subjected to this butchery—
Not left intact to charm a porch,
They'd carve and light her like a torch!

She told Gourdelia what she knew,
Both wondering what they ought to do—
And soon they hatched a clever plan,
As only pumpkin faeries can.

Gourdelia would roll on by
The wagon to distract the eye,
While Gourda crept up from behind
To save her sister by the rind.

Gordelia tumbled down the hill—
In truth, it gave her quite the thrill
To crunch across the fallen leaves,
And swerve around hay-bales and sheaves.

And Gourda, too, performed her part,
A-creeping near the pumpkin-cart,
While still the humans wondered how
A pumpkin rolled toward them now.

She snatched her sister quickly up,
And in her place, an acorn-cup
Was cast with glamour, so to seem
Just like a pumpkin from a dream.

She told Gourdette the frightful fate,
The dreadful end, that would await
If sadly she were taken back—
The lantern by the name of Jack.

She nearly fainted at the thought—
To think that she were almost caught!
But now the pretty pumpkins three
Were safe and happy as can be.

They huddled on their country hill,
Against October's twilight chill,
And watched the wagon roll away
Beneath the brilliant end of day.

The humans never saw the switch,
And joked it must have been a witch
Who sent the pumpkin tumbling down
The hill from off its grassy crown.

And as they disappeared from sight,
While distant windows winked with light,
Gourdelia, Gourda, and Gourdette
Recalled a day they'd not forget.

The Haunted House

There's a house on a hill at the end of the street
With two windows that watchfully flicker,
Where a pair of carved pumpkins on gateposts will greet
All who enter with many a snicker.

There are gravestones and leaves that fall over the lawn,
There are ravens that nest in the gables
Where the Hunter's Moon rises autumnal and wan—
It's a place of strange stories and fables.

Is the weather-vane whirling, or is that a witch
That is circling above the high tower?
Is that smoke-cloud or ghost seen to wiggle and twitch
From the chimney like milk that's gone sour?

I don't know, who can say, but we're headed its way
As we stop at each house trick-or-treating.
We will face all our fears of the house on this day,
Though it grins us a skeletal greeting...

II

HALLOWEEN DREAMS

The Haunted Pumpkin

There was a pumpkin kept apart
From all the others in the patch—
No children had it in their cart,
No chicken there would scratch.

It wore a spider-woven veil,
And shadows gathered where it sat.
Dead leaves arranged by evening's gale
Lay near it, lifeless, flat.

None dared to take this pumpkin home—
None dared to carve its evil face,
For fear some grim, autumnal gnome
Possessed it, trapped in place.

And still the haunted pumpkin rests
Beside a bat-infested oak,
Unrotted, as this tale attests,
Where weeds and lichens choke.

The Pumpkin Maiden

She grew amid the garden's tangled vines,
A pretty, pumpkin-colored manikin.
Of cucurbits the comely next of kin,
Both girl and gourd emerged with equal signs.

At Summer's End she reached her ripened shape,
And slowly woke from out her plant-like sleep,
But ere the farmer came his prize to reap,
The pumpkin maiden made her strange escape.

No longer tethered to the garden dirt,
She roamed afield, with long and leafy hair;
October's daughter, she had not a care
Except with bats and sprites to sport and flirt.

The scarlet sunset called her toward its glow—
Until a sudden umbrage barred her way:
Her viney hands played over husk and hay,
And soon she heard the cawing of a crow.

It was a scarecrow, someone like her kind,
And so she kissed his grinning pumpkin face—
Oh how she longed to more than gently trace
His carven brow with vision of the blind.

She found a sickle in the scarecrow's hand,
And carved herself a pair of almond eyes—
And silhouetted 'gainst the violet skies
Was her companion, splayed above the land.

But he was not a thing alive like her—
Already rot had crept into his heart.
The pumpkin maiden only could depart
Before that thing corruption made impure.

She took the candle from his laughing maw,
And caverned it within a mouth of woe;
And as the autumn winds began to blow,
She wandered onward through a waste of straw.

This was a world that promised only pain,
But there was beauty in the heart of night;
With forks of elf-fire flashing from her sight,
She watched a moon that reaped the starry grain.

She drank the night-wind through her eyes of fire,
And cast their flicker over cornfields dead.
She felt the flames grow strong in heart and head—
And yet her pumpkin limbs began to tire.

The gift of sight, that golden, fatal gift,
Had sped her journey down corruption's road;
To watch the swooping owl, the hopping toad,
The racing mice had cost a rotting rift.

At last the dawn, a cosmic marigold,
Began to blossom from behind the hill,
But as the world awoke, she fell so still—
Her squashy body crumbling unto mold.

Evil Harvest

The pumpkins rise from emerald mist,
On bodies of the risen dead;
Past vines and gravestones they persist,
Each revenant with pumpkin head.

A grinning witch-moon, poison-green,
Has pulled the corpses from their sleep,
To wander forth this Halloween
Wherever living vines may creep.

The pumpkins give them dim new life,
With vines that weave through skin and bone.
With them the autumn farms grow rife—
An evil harvest darkly sown.

For every jack-o'-lantern carved,
Another human life must fall—
For grim revenge the gourds are starved,
And from the pumpkin patch, they crawl.

DVS

Those Who Rise From Orange Slime

We rise from out the orange slime
Of pumpkin guts and stringy seed;
We come at the appointed time,
The night of Halloween to heed.

We do not live, but cannot die
Until our purpose is complete.
Beneath the late October sky,
We shamble down the lamplit street.

Each autumn squash you cruelly smash
Becomes our carved, half-crumpled face;
To snuff the jack-o'-lantern's flash
Ere midnight speeds our creeping pace.

All those who carelessly transgress
Against the rites of Halloween
Will know our cold and wet caress,
And nevermore again be seen.

The Harvester

He comes from the cornfield at first fall of dark,
With rusty old sickle and russet red cloak,
To take what is left him and follow the spark
Of flickering pumpkins while night-ravens croak.

A gourd or a corncob is all he requires,
A nut-cup of acorns, an apple, some cakes,
But they who would take the town elders for liars,
Ignoring old legends, will rue their mistakes.

The Harvester takes what a household can give—
When crops go unoffered, a life will suffice.
On All Hallows' Even, if all are to live,
'Tis better to pay him his portion, his price.

If ever such figure should come to your door
With basket of wicker while kids trick-or-treat,
'Tis best to remember the stories of yore,
And fill up his basket with many a sweet.

Invocation of the Pumpkin King

Harvest lord of living vine,
Waken from your tangled grave.
Cast on us your lantern-shine,
With your glow our path to pave.

Pumpkin King, we call you now,
To the present, from the past.
Carven-headed one, we vow
To be loyal till the last.

DVS

The Harvest Spirit

It whispers with a voice of straw
And withered leaves, the hissing wind;
It whispers with a pumpkin maw
To tell us that the veil has thinned.

It flickers in the yellowed corn,
Through golden sheaves its face has grinned—
The harvest spirit roams till morn
To tell us that the veil has thinned.

Halloween Dreams

I dream of the night
When witches take flight,
With lamps made of pumpkins to guide them
Above the black trees,
Where sunbeams yet tease
The eye, though the boughs soon will hide them.

I dream of the day
Not far down the way—
October's gold gateway awaits us...
Black cats will cause dread
When apples burn red,
The future what destiny fates us.

October's Eve

The twilight comes on quicker,
September takes her leave
As candles softly flicker
Upon October's Eve.

With wreath and gourd the porches
A rustic charm achieve,
While lanterns glow like torches
Upon October's Eve.

The moon, a silver sliver,
The harvest soon will cleave.
Dead leaves begin to shiver
Upon October's Eve.

The autumn mushrooms blossom,
Grimalkins lurk and weave;
Now wakes the weird and awesome
Upon October's Eve.

DVS

I'll Return In Late October

I'll return in late October,
When my grave is flecked with leaves,
And my name has nearly vanished
Where the ivy slowly weaves.

I'll return in late October,
When a crimson sunbeam falls
On a tomb that time has banished,
Where a somber raven calls.

I'll return in late October,
When a harvest gift is left
By a poet ghosts have guided
To my grave, forlorn, bereft.

I'll return in late October,
Like a phantom in your dreams,
When the witch has moon-ward glided,
And the jack-o'-lantern gleams.

Forever October

Forever October,
Forever the fields
Of corn that enrobe her,
Her scythe and its yields.

Forever her orchard
Where apples are piled
By trees that are tortured
By twilight winds wild.

Forever her flurries
Of fallen dead leaves;
Her field-mouse that scurries
Past acorns and sheaves.

Forever October,
Our fair golden queen,
A pumpkin her globe, her
High court Halloween.

October Thirty-First

The calendar at last says thirty-one,
And such a strange, fey magic fills the air;
It seems a veil's been drawn across the sun,
And there are ghosts and witches everywhere.

I've waited all year long for Halloween,
But now I almost don't know what to do—
Here is the haunted, charmed, autumnal scene
I long have dreamed of coming strangely true.

I carve the jack-o'-lanterns, choose my mask,
And pour the candy in an antique bowl;
I must accomplish an unspoken task—
The ancient rites are stirring in my soul.

I celebrate as best as I know how,
Giving my thanks for harvests large and small;
And in the blackest hour of night, I bow
Before an altar laid for those who call.

DVS

Halloween Carnival

The brightly painted wooden stands
Are selling cider, donuts, cakes.
We wander through enchanted lands
As twilight's witching spell awakes.

Our path is lined by hay-bales piled
With pumpkins, gourds of every kind—
Again I have become the child
From years I long thought left behind.

The carnival has many games,
And there are fortunes yet to tell,
But we pursue the faerie flames
Of jack-o'-lanterns and their spell.

They take us to a hidden nook,
A colored altar for the dead;
We write our names in time's red book—
Another chapter yet unread.

Halloween Acrostic

Hay-bales are piled with pumpkins, husks of corn
Add autumn charm all down the darkened street;
Lit candles flicker in a wind forlorn.

Like witches dressed, and devils, or the dead,
October's children come to trick-or-treat,
With burlap sacs for candied apples red.

Eventually, dead leaves go blowing down
Enshadowed roads, where jack-o'-lanterns greet
Night's moonlit silence with extinguished frown.

Halloween Shrine

Strange pumpkin-headed idols,
Noise-makers, candy-pails,
Orange books with gilded titles—
This shelf could tell some tales.

From countless childhoods taken,
Their owners now are dead.
Once all but lost, forsaken,
I cherish them instead.

The Hallowe'en Spirit
Streams off them like a flame;
It cheers me when I'm near it—
Old magic I reclaim.

A witch's night-black candle
Gives off its ghostly fire;
As devotee and vandal—
I light the summer's pyre.

III

AUTUMN
MEMORIES

Orange

Color of sunsets, pumpkins, and the flames
That glow in twilight houses' window-frames—
Of memories from autumns dimmed by time,
Whose phantoms fade to sepia, past their prime.

They of Little Faith

They haven't knelt at autumn shrines
Where leaves on silent evenings fall,
To spill the spicy, scarlet wines
In honor of the harvest doll.

They haven't roamed the pumpkin patch
For hours on lost October days
To find the lantern that could catch
The sunset and return its rays.

They haven't heard the great horned owl,
Nor known the omens it portends—
They wait to don the orange cowl
Until the time when summer ends.

They haven't kept the ancient faith,
Nor sown the harvest, mown the grain,
Nor have they known the deep hiraeth
For autumns men cannot attain.

Samhain Prayer

Samhain spirits, hear my prayer,
Spirits tongued with pumpkin-flare,
Tell me what the wind would whisper
After purple fall of vesper.

Samhain spirits, hear my call,
Autumn is not far at all;
Guide me to the end of summer,
Where the golden days grow glummer.

Samhain spirits, hear my vow
To abide by scythe and plow;
Let my fields be not fallow,
I who light the witch's tallow.

Samhain spirits, hear my prayer,
Spirits tongued with pumpkin-flare,
Tell to me the inner meaning
Of the mournful raven's keening.

Pumpkins

Emblems of autumn and of harvest time,
Symbols of bounty on the verge of dearth,
No greater gift has risen from the earth
Than humble pumpkins in their ripened prime.

With colors matching dead, decaying leaves,
And withered stems that twist like barren boughs,
Their carven faces whisper hallowed vows
The ancient Celts once took on certain eves...

They bring to mind the lurid, orange flames
That burned on Samhain 'gainst the black of night;
Their rinds remind us of the dying light
Of Summer's End, the day of many names.

They represent, at last, the fallen sun,
And are the lanterns that will keep its spark,
To guide our footsteps through the pathless dark
That at October's end has now begun.

DVS

Sunflowers

Sunflowers rise to mark the summer's height,
And hail the sun upon his golden throne—
But soon will come the time of rot and blight,
The sun replaced by autumn's moon of bone.

The sun will fall, and yet his flowers remain
As testament to his forgotten rule;
Like skeletons as parched as sun-bleached grain,
They sway in twilight winds grown cold and cruel.

With burnt and blackened faces, withered crowns,
The nodding liches watch their season's death;
The leaves that turn to yellows, reds, and browns,
Blown o'er the lawns as by a witch's breath.

Like yellow-petalled cenotaphs, they stand
As silent monuments to summer's end—
Yet in their death, they lift the faded brand
Of yesterday, where summer's dream can mend.

One More Golden Summer

Just one more golden summer,
Just one more tryst with youth,
Ere autumn's orange glimmer
Gives way to crimson truth.

Just one last sunlit season,
Ere twilight days should fade,
And I have my liaison
With the mower-maiden's blade.

Corn Moon

The Corn Moon, with a yellow glow,
Beams down to bless the pumpkin patch.
September breezes blow,
And in decaying leafage catch
Like words of woe.

The harvest time is now at hand,
When witching scarecrows yield their corn.
The farmer works his land
By moonlight till the come of morn,
As nature planned.

DVS

Autumn Memories

They come on filmy, fragile, gauzy wings
That catch the sunset lancing through the trees—
From faerie realms, these autumn memories
Sometimes return on haunted evenings.

Like falling leaves with silent whirl and twirl,
But drifting wistfully through windless air,
They linger for a moment in the glare—
Then disappear beyond the creek-bed's purl.

October Song

The song of October is silence,
The faraway call of the crow,
The hiss of the wind in its violence,
The leaves as they wither and blow.

The song of October is sorrow,
The heartbroken apples that fall,
The tears we'll be weeping tomorrow
In mourning a porcelain doll.

Pumpkin Grinning by the Gate

Pumpkin grinning by the gate,
Though the night is growing late,
Will you guard my hearth and home
From the shades that wayward roam?

Pumpkin glowing on the post,
Keep me safe from witch and ghost
As the leaves go blowing by,
And the wind begins to sigh.

The Season

This is the season when the trees
Begin to grin like russet skulls—
When all is stricken with disease,
And buzzing are the beehives' hulls.

This is the time when scarecrows watch
The yellowed, wide, and withered fields—
When reapers add another notch
To rusted scythes in name of yields.

This is the autumn, when the moon
Soars mournfully beyond our reach—
When distant owls sadly croon
A tragic, secret truth to teach.

This is the season summer warned
Would come when darker grew the days—
When cheer and childhood would be mourned
Amid the harvest fire's blaze.

When All Seems Lost

When all seems hopeless, all seems lost,
And you can't seem to find your way,
Just follow that far lantern tossed
In autumn winds, through woodlands gray.

Old Jack-o'-Lantern knows the trail,
The hidden road we need to find—
His lantern shines beyond the veil,
And dimly gleams on what's designed.

However tricksome it may seem,
Whichever way the pathway wends—
Through darksome grove, o'er mossy stream—
The puckish sprite knows where it ends.

When all seems hopeless, all seems lost,
Just take your pumpkin-lamp in hand,
For soon your luck will be uncrossed,
And one day—you will understand.

The Twelve Hallows

Twelve hallows for the hours,
Twelve hallows for the year,
The manifested powers
Of autumn, they appear.

In orange robes they gather
One late October eve,
When windy is the weather,
And woodland shades deceive.

A single jack-o'-lantern
Has summoned them this night—
The only ones who can turn
The seasons' wheel aright.

In worship of the pumpkin,
They walk their clockwise round,
Around the oaken stump, kin
Of he who has been crowned.

Harvest Home

The voice of wind that howls through carven teeth
Of lighted pumpkins summons me to come
And kneel before the oak-enwoven wreath
That decorates the rustic Harvest Home.

A hooded figure robed in orange greets
Me at the door, and decks me with my crown.
Where in my youth I might have begged for treats,
Now I must leave behind my life and town.

Chrysanthemums and gaudy marigolds
Adorn the table like a loved one's bier,
While all around me, in their faceless folds,
Twelve hallows gather to renew the year.

A candle burns before each gathered sage,
And yet their flames betray no ghost of breath.
An orange book lies open to a page
Whereon are rhymes of childhood's end, and death.

I am the thirteenth to attend the feast,
And soon am seated at the table's head.
My back is turned toward the darkened east
As we hold silent supper for the dead.

At last the chimes of midnight take their toll,
Extinguishing a candle with each strike—
Whereat each cloak collapses round a skull
That is a pumpkin, bone and gourd alike.

Where Yet October Dwells

Amidst the bleak advances of November,
There is a hollow lost in hidden dells,
Where yet a pumpkin keeps October's ember—
A place of dreams and spells.

It is a realm of gold and orange magic,
An autumn fastness, timeless, far away,
Whose aching beauty strikes the heart as tragic
With sunlight's fading ray.

No leaf there falls, the acorns cling to branches,
The waterwheel has stopped, the stream has stilled;
The sun, or moon, in haunted stillness blanches;
The grain has gone unmilled.

The only movement is the witchful flicker
A jack-o'-lantern casts across red leaves,
From off a frame of yellowed straw and wicker
To guide whoever believes.

Amidst the bleak advances of November,
There is a hollow lost in hidden dells—
A secret place I always will remember,
Where yet October dwells.

November Moon

A tinge of orange lingers,
Though carven features fade;
The trees, with gnarled fingers,
Reach out, distraught, dismayed.

The pumpkin moon they'd hailed
In rich October's realm
Has shrunken and has paled,
A skull o'er oak and elm.

AFTERWORD

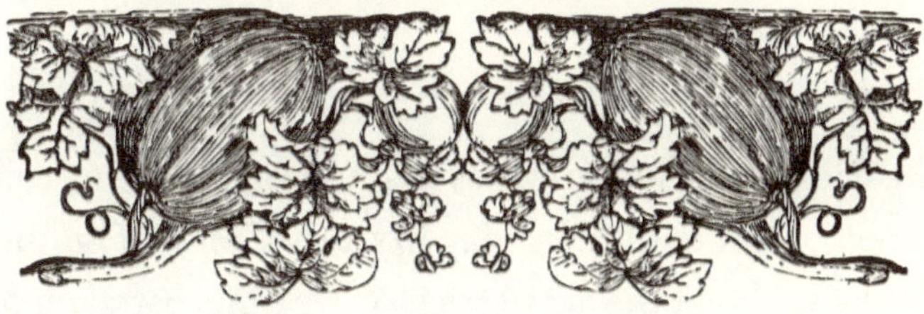

TRICK-OR-TREAT AS INITIATORY RITE, AND ATTENDANT SYMBOLISM

If it can be said that the most zealous devotees of Halloween collectively participate in a sort of modern-day Mystery Cult or Tradition, then it can also be said that the act of trick-or-treating, partaken of before we are truly able to appreciate its underlying transformative power or gnosis, is the initiatory rite at the heart of this tradition, the central act through which all of the hallowed lore and symbolism of Halloween are imparted to the young aspirant. This tradition, filtered through my own subjective lens, forms the basis for the autumnal mythology that informs much of my poetry, so here I will attempt to make a reckoning of it for all who would seek to gain a deeper insight into my writings.

As I see it, there are five archetypal figures in the mystery play of Halloween: The Witch, Devil, Ghost, Skeleton, and Jack-o'-Lantern—the quintessential fifth figure binding them all together. Together, these masked players enact the ritual of trick-or-treat, ultimately gaining initiation at the Haunted House—the archetypal dilapidated manse on the hill featured in so much Halloween art, literature, and films, to which trick-or-treaters are afraid to venture, but which yields the greatest reward to those who dare confront its creaking door. This door represents the Veil itself, which grows so thin at Hallowtide, and the glimpse beyond it into a dark and unfamiliar house, which occurs when the door opens and treats are dropped from a wizened hand into bags and buckets, represents a traversing of the Veil, and a gaining of secret wisdom. The candy itself may be said to symbolize this wisdom or boon, a literal reward hidden in a veiling wrapper, which is gained only after this doorstep confrontation with fear and the unknown (Perhaps, to take it even further, the pinwheel swirl found on many images of Halloween lollipops or suckers may represent the Labyrinth, and having attained the knowledge at its center). Lastly, this candy may be given out by a figure cloaked in an orange robe; this symbolizes the Hallowed One, or simply, a Hallow—the highest role that can be attained in this system, the Hierophant who presides over and preserves the Mysteries. It is their role to recreate the Haunted House of their youth, through whatever atmospheric decorations they see fit, and to distribute candy from its shadowed facade, thereby completing and continuing the sacred cycle.

What exactly the five archetypal figures of Halloween stand for is a complex and multilayered matter reaching back into antiquity, and spanning innumerable cultures and traditions, but I will give their basic associations here, as I interpret them. Furthermore, in a flight of inspiration, I have taken the liberty of carefully assigning to each of them an elemental association, so as to facilitate their incorporation as symbols into a broad range of spiritual or metaphysical systems.

THE WITCH: The Supernatural. Magic and witchcraft. Element: WATER, as exemplified by the potion being stirred in her cauldron.

THE DEVIL: Wicked powers. Danger. Trickery. Element: FIRE, as exemplified by his searing hot trident.

THE GHOST: The Dead. The distant past. Element: AIR, as exemplified by his fluttering white winding-sheet.

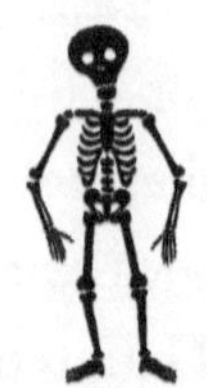

THE SKELETON: Death. Mysteries of the Underworld. Natural processes. Element: EARTH, as exemplified by his buried coffin.

THE JACK-O'-LANTERN: Traversing the Veil. Finding your way. Protection. Tradition and festivity. The harvest. Element: SPIRIT, as exemplified by the communal Halloween spirit kept alive in his flickering flame. This figure may appear simply as a carved pumpkin lantern, or as someone wearing a pumpkin mask or having a pumpkin head.

* * *

Like any arbitrary symbolic system, this is an imperfect, albeit carefully thought out one. There are of course many more characters to be found in modern day Halloween symbolism—the werewolf, the vampire, the zombie, to name a few—but I would argue that these characters can each be reduced or simplified or broken down as originating from one or more of the five archetypal figures. The vampire, for example, might be seen as a variation on the Skeleton or Ghost—one more soul from the ranks of the undead. Too, he could be associated with the Witch—a creature of the supernatural. Owls, bats, black cats, toads, spiders—all are incorporated into Halloween symbolism due to their association with the Witch, as her familiars. The scarecrow might be said to be an incarnation of the Jack-o'-Lantern, him being a harvest figure often having a pumpkin head, or at least residing in a pumpkin patch. Furthermore, the archetypal Ghost and Skeleton could be combined into simply one figure to represent the dead—perhaps a specter with a grinning skull beneath its billowing hood—yielding a set of just four archetypal figures. Some might go further still and omit the Devil, having lumped him in with the Witch as another being from the supernatural or non-human realm.

Again, this is an imperfect system, as even the best system is, and the reader is free to adapt it to their own personal use or preference as they see fit. As I have given it here, this is simply the model that has naturally arisen from my writings, imagination, and ruminations, which has in turn further informed my poems, and the mythic lens through which I view and think about Halloween.

POEM NOTES

Pumpkin Country

For me, Pumpkin Country is a real place—the annual pumpkin patch
held at Irvine Regional Park, in Orange, California. Every year, it opens
in mid-September—just a few days after my birthday. So many of my
poems are at least partly inspired by my many annual trips to this lovely
park. I even proposed to my fiancée there (albeit in late August), beside
one of several historical memorials overlooking the sprawling lake ("I
want you to always be the one who goes with me to the pumpkin patch,"
I said...) Whenever I pass from this plane—may it be a long, long time
from now—if I am given a choice of places to haunt, it well might be that
park—Pumpkin Country. Look for me there, readers of the far future—
look for me there, on an October evening, when the sun slants a certain
way, and the leaves are peculiarly restless. Look for me where a lone
pumpkin rests, seemingly at random, in a place of potency. You will find
me there, a wraith—the Spirit of Halloween, eternal guardian of our high
holiday; friend to the chosen, foe to all who would snuff out the jack-o'-
lantern flame.

Carver's Rhyme

I spontaneously came up with this rhyme while preparing to carve a
pumpkin in poet Adam Bolivar's backyard. This was the very same
pumpkin that had been found in a field on Sauvie Island, and which
would later serve as a drink-ticket-dispensing centerpiece of the
Hippocampus Happy Hour, hosted by Derrick Hussey, at the H. P.
Lovecraft Film Festival in Portland, Oregon.

The Parade Lantern

Antique Halloween parade lanterns are among the most highly sought
after (and expensive) items for collectors of vintage Halloween ephemera.
They feature a small tin jack-o'-lantern, wherein a candle can be placed,
which is mounted on a stick for carrying. I'd sure like to own one, one
day...

Crepe Paper Patterns

Halloween—more than any other holiday—seems to revel in an almost freakish repetition of its cherished symbols—pumpkins, witches, black cats, moons, stars, spiders, autumn leaves, ghosts, skeletons, and on, and on, and on... You will see garlands hung with a hundred pumpkin cutouts; tablecloths utterly crawling with black cats and spiders; and—perhaps most delightfully obnoxious of all—vintage Halloween crepe paper displaying an endlessly repeating spooky scene. I take my cue from such décor, shamelessly using these same symbols over and over in my imagery.

Appalachian Halloween

For whatever reason, though I haven't yet been there, I've long had a fascination with Appalachia. A certain mystique surrounds that mountainous region—indeed, it is one of the most wild and heavily forested areas in the continental United States. Being the dark cauldron of obscure folklore and cryptozoological research that it is, I thought I ought to write a poem celebrating Appalachian Halloween, so I did some research and wove together some of the peculiar folk customs observed in that region.

Cat-o'-Lantern

In the past couple of years, I've noticed that jack-o'-lanterns bearing cat faces seem to be becoming more common, and I've also learned that they are colloquially called cat-o'-lanterns, so I felt compelled to write a fantastical poem celebrating them. This increase in popularity could possibly be due to the resurgence of vintage Halloween style in modern décor. Acquiring a lovely plastic cat-o'-lantern from the local grocery store a couple Octobers ago was ultimately the *cat*-alyst for writing this poem, and some of the imagery in it was inspired by a vintage Halloween postcard depicting several black cats in red pointed caps tiptoeing by on two legs, late at night... Similarly, I've noticed that what I've taken to calling owl-o'-lanterns are fairly popular as well, and last year I carved my first one, from a self-grown pumpkin. It may be that I will write an Owl-o'-Lantern poem in the future...

Witch's Candy

For some reason, the image of a swirly, black and orange lollipop with a bow wrapped around it is potent with meaning for me. It seems emblematic of so much—almost as quintessentially a Halloween symbol as the omnipresent jack-o'-lantern. My love of spiral motifs and specifically swirly lollipops is so strong that my artist signature on my artworks, KAO, always bears a spiral in the O, to be reminiscent of a swirly Halloween lollipop and all it stands for—fun, sweetness, mischief—trick-or-treat! In fact, I tend to like fun depictions of all kinds of candy in art—especially Halloween candy—so it is a recurring element in my poetry and art.

The Haunted Pumpkin

I have long had the idea of every pumpkin patch containing a certain, special pumpkin—perhaps more perfect than all the others, or perhaps more sinister... When we go to the pumpkin patch, we look for the exact right pumpkin that was meant for us to take home, but what if there is also a pumpkin that should be avoided at all costs—lurking at the edge of the patch, in that liminal space where carefully arranged gourds thin out among the creeping weeds, and the trees cast a deeper shadow, and the laughter of children sounds muted, as if filtered through an unseen veil...?

October's Eve

It seems to me that October's Eve ought to be a recognized holiday— the last night before the kingdom of October once again unfurls in gold and orange splendor. It is a night pregnant with expectation, a transitory night when the normal, everyday world fades away into a long-awaited dream; when, once again, we return home—to October. This poem was based on an actual stroll I took on October's Eve around my neighborhood a couple of years ago.

October Thirty-First

In addition to being Halloween, the day of October Thirty-First is also just that—a day on the calendar—one day, albeit a very special one. I find that thinking in terms of the calendrical date has a slightly different shade of meaning than the word Halloween. It encompasses the whole day, from morning to night, whereas many people focus on the twilight hours when thinking of Halloween. On this day, in the morning especially, I often feel a peculiar anxiety—a sense that there is much to do, and little time to prepare—a sense of wonderment and bafflement that the Great Day is actually here! This poem attempts to encapsulate these nebulous feelings. Preparing for Halloween and celebrating it fully is so important to me that I have recurring nightmares that it is late on Halloween night, and for whatever reason, I haven't prepared—I haven't done anything to observe the Great Day. In the latest version, I had ten pumpkins, but hadn't carved a single one (though one of them had grown in the actual shape of a jack-o'-lantern, hollow in the middle, face and all, with no exposed flesh, every surface being sealed by rind, even on the inside). Even the entire year isn't enough to plan and prepare for Halloween, and I think I will only be fully initiated into its Mystery when I pass from this plane, or am very near to doing so. If my life can be said to have a purpose, figuring out how to celebrate the perfect Halloween—trying time and time again, year after year—could easily be a central part of it.

Halloween Carnival

This poem is directly based on a visit to Pumpkin Nights, a few years ago, at the Los Angeles County Fairgrounds. This annual October event consists of a winding path lined by thousands of (artificial) carved pumpkins twinkling in the twilight, arranged into fantastical displays and even sculptures (a gigantic dragon made of pumpkins is one of the famous yearly fixtures). The experience is divided into several themed lands, and often special pumpkins hidden in each land will spell out a message, that—when repeated to an attendant at the end—will earn one a special prize (mine was a button bearing a sugar skull design). In the Dia de los Muertos-themed area, we each wrote the name of some deceased relatives on a slip of paper, to adorn a colorful wall—the Ofrenda—and I was taken aback by how emotional the experience was for me. I felt the spirit of my departed relatives live again, for a brief moment of remembrance. Even as simple a gesture as it was, I was nearly reduced to tears by the power of the experience.

The Harvest Spirit

The words to this poem came to me on the day of Halloween itself, as I drowsed on my bed for a midday nap, listening to the wind whispering outside my open window, telling secret things, weaving pictures invisible to the eye, but dimly seen in waking dream.

Halloween Shrine

As I believe I've mentioned before, I have a Halloween Shrine that I keep set up all year long, and this poem is directly based on it. It is a strange thing to ruminate on the probability that the former owners of my more vintage items may well be dead by now (I'd like to think that they are pleased by the care with which I preserve their childhood treasures). I often hold my coveted first edition copy of *The Book of Halloween*, by Ruth Edna Kelley, and try to imagine the hands that have held it, the autumnal dreams that have been dreamt while poring over its October lore, its tales of Halloweens past. It is very tempting to list every item that adorns my shrine, but I will list just one more special piece in my collection—a vintage jack-o'-lantern candy-pail purchased in an antique store in St. Helens, Oregon, also known as 'Halloweentown,' where the beloved movie series was filmed.

Orange

This poem was originally supposed to appear in the first section of *Past the Glad and Sunlit Season,* directly after the poem "Waiting for October," and preceding the poem "Orange Gleams," but somehow, by some autumnal goblinry, it was left out. I only just now discovered this minor mishap, a full year later, while working on my introductory text for this book... In it, I mention the fact that together, the two books comprise one hundred poems. Well, I figured I had better recount the poems in the first book, so as to be certain of the accuracy of my statement—and I only counted fifty-four poems, whereas I had been certain there were fifty-five. A careful comparison of the physical book with my original manuscript eventually revealed to me the unexpected omission. I am very pleased to include the missing poem in this book instead, so that it will not be forever lost, as it easily could have been.

The Season

This poem, oddly enough, was inspired by a brief stint working in an e-commerce warehouse. The job ended up being an absolutely terrible fit for me, and I quit after just three days (thankfully, I was able to return to my previous job!). While there, a coworker said something to me along the lines of, "Just wait until *The Season...*" (in reference to the holiday season—their busiest time). Well, mandatory sixty hour weeks sounded like a death sentence to me, so I got out well before The Season could arrive. It was a dark hour in my life—a time when I'd clearly taken a wrong turn—and so this poem was born. Some poems come at a cost, and this was definitely one of them. Lastly, fun fact—the reference to 'trees grinning like skulls' was inspired by an actual tree I saw one evening during October whose foliage, when viewed by twilight from the exact right angle, looked just like a skull. I had the occasion to walk past this tree again the other day, for the first time in two years, and I am happy to report that it still looks vaguely like a skull. It resides in Disneyland, as seen from the Esplanade.

They of Little Faith

This poem was a reaction to an increasingly prevalent attitude toward or approach to celebrating Halloween that some folks seem to have. They think that just keeping decorations out and watching horror movies makes them some kind of special Halloween devotee. That's all well and good, but you and I know that there is more to devoting oneself to the Ways of Halloween—so much more. Halloween, to me, is the most sacred day of the year—and I do mean sacred, in the full and true sense of the word. Absolutely nothing is more important than observing the ancient ways of this high harvest festival. To prepare for it is a matter spanning the entire year; the seeds are planted in spring, the dream nourished through summer. Never does the jack-o'-lantern flame waver in my heart; never is my soul unmisted by an October yearning. The harvest must be observed, the chants must be spoken, the rites must be enacted. I would die in the name of Halloween; and upon my deathbed, Halloween will be in my thoughts, as I travel to the Otherworld, already planning my Return. That is my long-winded and poetic way of saying— Halloween is really, really important to me—as important and integral to one's soul and identity as anything can be—and I take umbrage at the modern idea that Halloween is some kind of mere surface level celebration, a facade of décor and candy. Halloween is the time of Spirits, and we must look beyond the Veil to attain the rewards given to the truly faithful.

One More Golden Summer

For some reason, every summer, I get the idea in my head that that summer will be the last one I can ever truly enjoy, before the larger responsibilities of advancing adulthood set in. I feel it will be my last "innocent" summer, where a fleeting flicker of childhood yet dances in the grass... Every year so far, however, I have been proven wrong. I am starting to think that I will always find a certain carefree joy in the summertime, no matter what, and that for me, my childhood will never truly end. The dark season always comes, and my own mortal years ever advance, yet the light half of the year will always return. The golden summer will always be there.

Sunflowers

Sunflowers are one of my favorite things to grow in my garden—the pumpkin patch never feels quite complete without those large, leonine flowers flaming above the sprawling green leaves of the pumpkin vines. This poem is inspired by my meditations on the towering black husks that remain, after their prideful torches have burnt out—after their petals have been scattered on the hot late summer wind, to be lost among the weeds like shriveled rays of errant sunlight. The summer does not disappear; the summer never truly ends. It remains. It rots—but its ghost remains.

Pumpkin Grinning By the Gate

This poem celebrates the jack-o'-lantern as a protective or apotropaic symbol. The infamous coronavirus pandemic continued to be in full swing during October 2020, and Halloween again felt like a truly dangerous night, just as it was regarded to be in olden times. A very real threat stalked the night—the specter of death and disease was a presence more strongly felt than is even normal on Halloween. But despite the plague ravaging the land, Halloween prevailed. Where some folks lamented that Halloween would be canceled, others constructed candy chutes—decorated tubes, often adorned with stripes and colored lights, that could slide candy down into the buckets of trick-or-treaters from a safe distance of more than six feet. I got to use one of these chutes myself, and it was the highlight of my night—alongside the candy-corn flavored Jello shots I got across the street (relax—these were for adults only!) Treat tables set up near the curb were a pandemic Halloween staple as well, allowing trick-or-treaters to choose their own treats from the table, at a safe distance from the homeowners, who would wave and wish intrepid passers-by a Happy Halloween.

Harvest Home

Despite having the same title, this poem has nothing to do with Thomas Tryon's novel of the same name (I hadn't even heard of it or read it at the time, though I have read it since). Just as I imagine Tryon did, I simply named my poem after the old folk tradition of Harvest Home, which I have long been intrigued by. Much like Summer's End, I find the phrase Harvest Home to be very evocative and suggestive, stirring up deep memories and half glimpsed secrets, so I tried to write something that conveys the imagery and overall atmosphere this bewitching phrase seems to conjure in my subconscious mind.

The Twelve Hallows

I first envisioned the Twelve Hallows while meditating at midnight one Halloween. I wanted to see what kind of images might appear in my mind during such an activity, done at such an auspicious time, and the image of twelve orange-hooded individuals gathering in the woods by night, around a lone jack-o'-lantern, was one of the first and possibly most intriguing images to appear to me. Why there were twelve, I did not exactly know, though I have intuited that each one presides over one of the twelve months of the year. On Halloween, a thirteenth Hallow is chosen, since the twelve from the previous year symbolically die or are removed from office at this time. The thirteenth Hallow must preside over this harvest ceremony, and lead the proceedings into a new year. None of this information has any credible source—unless you count my poetic intuition as such a thing. These are all things I have imagined or "made up," while immersing myself in the energetic currents of the season. To me, they are real in an abstract, symbolical way; part of my personal lore, the fabric from which I weave my own ceremonial mythology.

Pumpkins

The symbol of the pumpkin is so important and ubiquitous in American culture that I decided to explore what they mean and symbolize to me, personally. The mere sight of a pumpkin always seems to fill me with joy—especially when I see the first pumpkins arriving in stores, or when I make my first trip to the pumpkin patch in September—so I wanted to take the ultimate close-up look at everything a pumpkin seems to stand for and make me feel on a subconscious level. I am tempted to expound upon the matter, but I think my poem has already done that! I was largely inspired to write this poem by reading a certain chapter on pumpkin obsession in *Halloween Nation* by Lesley Pratt Bannatyne— I highly recommend all of her books. And while I'm at it, be sure to read all of Lisa Morton's books as well!

Where Yet October Dwells

When October is over, and the candles have sputtered out within the rotting yellow caverns of tired jack-o'-lanterns, I always become deeply nostalgic for Halloween—so near, yet so far. It may have occurred only the night before, but now, sadly, an entire year separates us from that special day. My heart always tells me that Halloween is more than a day—that it is a way of life, and that it is—perhaps—a place, just over yonder hill, in some sleepy hollow... Halloween never truly ends—it never truly leaves us. For it is in us that the jack-o'-lantern flame forever abides. This poem imagines such a shadowed, sheltered place where Halloween might yet abide against the advances of November—a timeless, pastoral pocket of existence where time is frozen, and our memories may yet live again.

ABOUT THE CONTRIBUTORS

K. A. OPPERMAN is a poet and artist hailing from southern California. In addition to his Halloween poetry, Opperman is the author of two volumes of Gothic poetry: *The Crimson Tome* (2015) and *The Laughter of Ghouls* (2021), both published by Hippocampus Press. His work has appeared in *Midnight Under the Big Top* (Cemetery Dance Publications, 2020), *Black Wings of Cthulhu 6* (Titan Books, 2018), *Spectral Realms, Vastarien, Weirdbook, Weird Fiction Review, The Audient Void, Eye to the Telescope*, and many other venues.

ADAM BOLIVAR is a poet of dark fantasy, a writer of weird fiction, and a marionette playwright with a particular interest in balladry and "Jack" tales—a folkloric tradition centered on a trickster-hero that dates back to medieval times and was preserved in isolated reaches of the Appalachian Mountains. His poetry has appeared in the pages of such publications as *Spectral Realms* and *Black Wings of Cthulhu*. "The Rime of the Eldritch Mariner," his ballad combining Coleridge's *The Rime of the Ancient Mariner* with Lovecraft's "The Call of Cthulhu," won a Rhysling Award for long-form poetry. His collection of weird balladry and Jack tales, *The Lay of Old Hex*, was published by Hippocampus Press in 2017 and was nominated for the Bram Stoker Award. His book of occult detective tales, *The Ettinfell of Beacon Hill*, was recently published by Jackanapes Press. His second collection of poetry, *Ballads for the Witching Hour*, is forthcoming from Hippocampus Press in 2022.

DAN SAUER is a graphic designer and artist living in Oregon. In 2016, he co-founded (with editor/publisher Obadiah Baird) *The Audient Void: A Journal of Weird Fiction and Dark Fantasy*, which features his design and illustration work. Since 2017, he has worked extensively on book covers and interior art for Hippocampus Press and other publishers. His art often takes the form of surreal collage and photomontage, as pioneered by artists such as Max Ernst, Wilfried Sätty, Harry O. Morris and J. K. Potter.

Book of Shadows
Grim Tales & Gothic Fancies

For those who hunger for small bites of horror sweetened with black humor, this collection of Grim Tales and Gothic Fancies offers a satisfying repast: morbidly playful riffs on the faerie tales of the Brothers Grimm; darkly exquisite Gothic fables in both prose and verse; and hell-raising evocations of beings both demonic and diabolic. A rich feast of horrors leavened with wit, *Book of Shadows* offers a delicious glimpse into the decadent heart and mordant mind of Manuel Arenas.

"The poetry and fables of Manuel Arenas are like specially gifted party favours on All Hallows Eve. Unwrap them and you are regaled with black humour shot through with light … elegant beauty one breath from decay …"

—**Galad Elflandsson**, Author of *The Black Wolf*

AVAILABLE NOW!

www.JackanapesPress.com
www.facebook.com/Jackanapes-Press

www.ingramcontent.com/pod-product-compliance
Lightning Source LLC
Chambersburg PA
CBHW030351200726
48286CB00013B/1077

9 781956 702040